DI

NINJA

SPY

5

Where evil goes, the ninja will follow…

Diary of a Ninja Spy 5: Alien Attack!

William Thomas

Peter Patrick

Also in the Diary of a Ninja Spy series:

Diary of a Ninja Spy

Diary of a Ninja Spy 2

Diary of a Ninja Spy 3

Diary of a Ninja Spy 4

Also by William Thomas and Peter Patrick:

Diary of a Super Spy

Diary of a Super Spy 2: Attack of the Ninjas!

Diary of a Super Spy 3: A Giant Problem!

Diary of a Super Spy 4: Space!

Diary of a Super Spy 5: Evil Attack!

Diary of a Super Spy 6: Daylight Robbery!

Chapter 1

Ugh.

I am *sooo* bored.

My best friend Fred is conducting one of his super special, but *super boring*, experiments. He loves this stuff.

"Let's go outside, Fred," I say to my friend. "We've been inside all day."

"No Blake, this is important! This is an advanced scientific experiment! This is one of the most important things I have ever done, and it may be one of the most important moments in history. If this works, then our lives may be changed forever. The *entire world* may be changed forever. You can go without me, but I need to finish this."

"I'll wait for you, Fred. You need to leave your room. Besides, I need a wingman for when we bump into Amy."

Amy is a girl at school that I like. I'm not being mean, but Fred is incredibly nerdy. When he is standing next to me, I look totally cool.

We are in Fred's bedroom, where he conducts most of his scientific experiments. Even though we don't have homework this weekend, Fred still does science for fun. Last week, he constructed a robot using only tissue boxes, an old computer, and four batteries, but that didn't go so well. All the robot did was laugh. He laughed particularly hard when he saw Fred's new haircut. Fred took the batteries out after that.

But the week before that, he built a super powerful computer made completely out of sticks and old electrical wire. He even invented his own game on it, called Minecrafty. It was like Minecraft, but more crafty. This kid is a genius.

Fred keeps tinkering away at whatever he is doing… wait a minute. What is he doing?

"Er, Fred?"

"Yes, Blake."

"What are you doing?" I ask.

"Are you serious!? Did you really just ask me that question? I have been talking about this for months. I have spent the whole day working on this project, with you next to me, and you ask me what am I doing? I have told you about a thousand times! Do you ever listen to me?!"

Hmmm, Fred seems frustrated.

"Ha, just joking, Fred. Of course, I know what you are doing. I totally know. I know so much about what you are doing that I should get an award for 'Most Knowingly Person Around.' If there is not an award for that, then we should make one. I could get the first award, and then the award would be named after me - 'The Blake Award for Knowing People.' Yep, that would work. Totally."

I don't know what Fred is doing.

I have no idea.

But I have good reasons for not listening to Fred ramble on about science all day, every day.

Firstly, I am not very good at science, and secondly, I have been very busy lately with my secret life as a Ninja Spy. I have been training and fighting, and training and fighting, and training and fighting, and eating hamburgers. And of course, there has also been training and fighting! I know. It's a lot of work.

Being a Ninja Spy isn't easy, but it's totally worth it.

There's lots of hardcore action and adventure every week. I have battled ninja ghosts, evil clones and the world's toughest bad guys!

In the past week, my trainer Tekato has been teaching me how to catch ninja stars. I haven't been able to catch one yet, but I am getting better at it.

And I still go to school every day.

Even though I am not allowed to reveal to anyone that I am a Ninja Spy, I love it. My closest friends know what I do, but to the rest of the world, my identity is secret.

And I haven't lost a ninja battle yet!

I'm unbeatable!

My name is Blake Turner, and I am the undefeated Ninja Spy!

This is me and my unofficial scoreboard.

There is no-one else at the Ninja Spy Agency who can boast about such a great record. And I've been sure to tell everyone. Well, as much as I can because I am sworn to secrecy.

"Yes! I've done it!" Fred yells in joy. "Blake, look! I've done it! I've made it work! I've hooked the green conductor to the earth wire, and the red velvet hammer to the blue shiny button. That will enable the electrical current to flow to the correct areas of the machine. Woo!"

"Yay?" I have no idea what he has done.

"I've completed my Intergalactic Communicator project!"

"Wow?" I still have no idea what he has done.

Fred starts to speak into a microphone, which is attached to his guitar amplifier, which is attached to his computer, which is then attached to a radar dish sitting at his bedroom window. The radar dish is pointed high in the sky.

His voice goes in the microphone, travels through his contraption and comes out as a high pitched scribbly sound at the other end.

"Hello, my friends. My name is Fred and I come in peace," Fred calmly says into his microphone. "If you are out there, please respond."

"Ha ha ha!" I blurt out.

"Are you trying to make contact with someone in the International Space Station? Is that what this is?! That's so cool! I would love to talk with the astronauts."

"No, Blake. This is a communicator... to talk to aliens!"

"Aliens?"

"Yes, Blake. Aliens."

"But aliens don't exist!"

"You're wrong, Blake. They do exist, and they will talk back to us. The device is sending my message deep, deep into outer space. My voice is traveling between galaxies, searching for aliens that can respond. They are out there, Blake. They will hear my voice and respond. I will be the first person on planet Earth to talk with aliens."

"You are just talking to the stars, you loony! You're totes crazy, Fred. What a waste of time! Come on, let's go outside," I say to Fred.

Fred sits up and smiles at me.

"You're right, let's go outside as a celebration of a successful experiment! Extraterrestrial life does exist, and I'll prove it to you when I get a response," Fred says with confidence. "I wonder what they will say? Maybe they will tell me the secrets of the universe, like how to time-travel. Or maybe they will teach me how to build an Intergalactic Spacecraft. Or maybe-"

"Or maybe they will teach you how to talk to girls."

"Um, yep," Fred responses. He isn't great at talking to girls. Last time he tried to talk with Gemma, the girl he likes, he couldn't even open his mouth. He spent five minutes just staring at her.

"Let's go," I pat Fred on the back.

"Sure, but first I need to wee," he announces.

As he leaves the room, I am left alone with his new experiment. I could totally send a better message to the non-existent aliens out there. I could tell them all about the Earth and how beautiful it is, or I could tell them all about the wonderful things that humans have accomplished…

Nah.

I grab his microphone and turn on the Intergalactic Communicator.

"Hello, aliens! My name is Blake, and I am the greatest Ninja Spy of all time! I am so great that I am undefeated in all my battles. I would easily kick butt against any aliens listening to this message. Aliens are stupid. Aliens are so dumb that aliens don't know they are dumb! And also, all your parties suck - they have no *atmosphere*! Ha-ha! And I know what an alien's favorite chocolate is – it's a Mars bar!"

"Blake! What are you doing?" Fred barges in. "Did you just taunt the entire galaxy with a stupid message? Who knows who is listening to that out there in space?"

"Nobody is out there, Blake. There is no such thing as aliens."

"Blake, aliens are out there. And this is *surely* going to come back and bite you on the butt!"

"Don't worry about it, Fred. Be cool. There is definitely, absolutely, positively no such thing as aliens. It is just something astronauts say to keep themselves in a job. There are no aliens out there listening to my message, and if they were, they would be too scared to come here and meet me," I reply with confidence.

Fred replies, "Blake, I have a feeling that you are wrong. Very wrong…"

Chapter 2

Before I get a chance to leave Fred's house and go outside, my Mom turns up.

This is bad. Why is she here?

I don't remember doing something wrong.

"Blake, why are you still here? Have you forgotten something?" Mom asks.

Mom knows *exactly* what I've forgotten. Mom likes to play games like that – I have enough tests at school, I don't need them from Mom as well. She is always asking me questions like that – 'Blake, did you leave your shirt on the floor?', 'Blake, did you clean up your dinner?', 'Blake, did you eat all the dog food again?'

"Uh, no. I remember," I reply to Mom, although I have no idea what she is talking about.

"Fred and I are just leaving to go to that thing… and do the other thing… for the thing."

"Oh good, you did remember. Why are you bringing Fred?" Mom asks.

I look at Fred, and he shrugs his shoulders.

"We are going to get you fitted for a suit for our family portraits. How exciting!" Mom jumps with joy. "This is the best day of the year!"

Aww, man! I hate these family portraits! Every year, we spent hours shopping, and Mom ends up buying me an ultra-embarrassing suit. Her taste in clothes is terrible!

And shopping for hours with my Mom is NOT a cool look for my image. It gets worse too - we spend hours posing for photos that go into an embarrassing family calendar, which Mom sends to everyone!

"So what have you boys been doing this morning?" Mom asks.

"Just solving the mysteries of the universe, Mrs. Turner," Fred responds. "And we are about to solve one of the universe's greatest questions."

"That sounds interesting. What is it? How to make Blake clean up his bedroom?" Mom laughs loudly.

Nice one, Mom.

"We are looking for aliens, Mrs. Turner," Fred responds. "Blake doesn't think they exist, but I am absolutely certain that they are out there. There is lots of evidence that they might exist, but nobody has proved it yet. So I built an Intergalactic Communicator, which will allow me to talk with any aliens out there. I've sent a message into space, and now I will just wait for them to respond. I'm sure there are aliens out there, and I would love to be able to talk to one."

"That's lovely," Mom smiles. "I am so glad that you boys are so responsible."

"Yeah. Responsible for defending the world…" I whisper under my breath, so Mom doesn't hear.

Mom doesn't know that I am a Ninja Spy.

She thinks that I spend most of my time playing at Fred's house, or doing my homework at the library, or walking our pet turtle.

Walking a pet turtle is hard.

Sometimes, it takes an entire day for the turtle to walk around the block. Luckily, I have a leash for him.

It can be hard defending the world against evil when Mom still wants you home for dinner.

"I met an alien once," Mom says calmly.

"What? Really? Where? When?" I am surprised.

"Oh… wait… no. That was your first-grade teacher – Mr. Fartybottom. He sure did look like an alien, though."

Yep. I always did think that Mr. Fartybottom was a weird looking guy. And those big, beady eyes sure were strange.

"But I did have a dream last night that I got into a fight with an alien," Mom says. "He was big and ugly, and I couldn't think of a way to defeat him. We were in a really intense battle, and he was so strong. It looked like I was about to be destroyed but then I figured out a way to defeat him."

"What did you do?" Fred asks.

"I reached out and grabbed a rope to lasso the alien. I swung the lasso around and caught him. Once he was tied up, I flipped him around and around, and then threw him back into outer space. I was so proud of myself. I defended the world against the alien attack."

Mom is so weird.

"Nice dream, Mom, but how could you lasso an alien? That is so dumb."

"Well," Mom smiles. "I think it would work. Quite often, dreams can give you clues about how to solve a problem. So if you ever get into a fight with an alien, just remember that you should lasso them, and then throw them back into outer space."

I shake my head, "Ugh, you are so embarrassing."

"Fred, would you still like to come to the family photo shot?" Mom asks.

"Oh, I just remembered something very important to do. I… have… to… um… wash my eyeballs with soap."

"Oh really?" Mom asks surprised.

"Yes, yes. very important. I do it once a week, just to make sure that my perfect vision stays perfect," Fred replies smiling. "It's really important to have perfect vision for my science experiments."

"Maybe you should try that, Blake?"

"I don't do science experiments, Mom. That's not my thing."

"Your room is a science experiment," Mom says.

"Ha ha!" Fred laughs and then gives my Mom a high-five.

"Don't high-five my Mom," I shake my head. "You are so embarrassing, Mom. Leave the jokes to me. There can only be one funny person in this family."

"You can be funny… funny-looking!" Mom laughs and high-fives Fred again.

"How humiliating," I mutter as I walk out of Fred's house.

"Bye Fred," Mom waves.

My Mom can be so embarrassing. At my basketball game last week, she came to the game dressed as a cheerleader with pom-poms and a sign that said, '*GO BAKE*.'

Clearly, she forgot the letter 'L' in my name, and the other team thought that she was telling them to go to the kitchen. Now everyone at school calls me 'Bake'. Thanks, Mom.

"Your friend Fred is nice," Mom remarks as we walk to the car.

"Yep. And a bit weird. He believes in aliens," I reply. "I am completely sure that there are no aliens out there and that he will get no response to the silly message that he sent out to the rest of the universe."

Yep. I am completely sure…

Chapter 3

When we arrive at the mall, Mom makes me try on so many different suits.

She wants the 'perfect' look for next year's family calendar. Mom spends hours trying to decide which style suits me best...

Um, none of them!

"Somebody has to set the trends, Blake. You shouldn't wear something because everyone else is wearing it. You should have your own personal style. That's very important."

"A leopard print suit will never be in style, Mom."

"Hmmm… yes. You are probably right about that one."

When Mom doesn't find the 'perfect' suit, we leave the mall and go to her favorite shop in the whole world. The shop isn't allowed to be in the mall and is at the edge of town. I have never, ever seen anyone else in the store except for Mom.

The store is called 'Ridiculous Men's Fashion.'

Mom says it's a French name, but I'm not so sure.

She often shops for Dad's birthday presents here. Last year, she bought him a suit for his birthday, but he looked more like a balloon than a man in a nice suit.

Just as I am trying on Mom's latest choice of horrible suits, I look to the entrance of the store. And then I see her.

Amy Cullen. AKA, The prettiest girl in school.

Walking right past the shop where I am getting my new suit fitted.

I am so excited to see Amy...

"Hi Amy," I shout, running out onto the street to say hello. "You look radical."

Agh! I meant to say radiant, not radical.

And then I realize that I am still wearing one of the ugly suits my Mom was making me try on!

"Ummm…. yeahhhhh…," she says, looking surprised to see me.

"Do you want to hang out? Maybe grab an ice-cream?" I say smiling, trying to look cool while still wearing the outrageous suit.

"Ummm... Maybe not. I've got a… um… thing… to do. Over there."

"Over where?"

"Over there…" she points into the distance. "Somewhere a long way away from here."

She moves a lot faster away from the store.

Oh man.

Why did she have to see me in my totally bad suit?

"Oh Sweetie, you look adorable," Mom says, kissing me on the cheek as I walk back into the store. "I bet that girl thought you looked amazing too. I love you, you little yum-yum!"

Great.

Mom says we'll buy the suit, and I feel too deflated to argue with her. I can't even be bothered getting changed back into my normal clothes.

After seeing me in this suit, Amy will never think I'm cool.

My chance with her is gone.

I have no idea where Mom got her taste in style from, but it is hideous. Truly hideous. I hope no one else ever, ever, ever sees me in this humiliating suit again.

Chapter 4

On the way home from the 'Ridiculous Men's Fashion' store, we drive past Fred's house. It's just around the corner from my place, and I usually walk between houses.

Fred is outside on his front lawn, yelling, and dancing. He isn't usually outside, and I have never seen him dance before. Actually, I am not even sure if he is dancing. He could just be doing some sort of tribal rain spell. Maybe he just wants it to rain.

But why is he so happy?

"Mom! Stop the car! I've got to see Fred," I say to Mom. "There must be something happening! He looks very excited!"

As soon as she stops the car, I jump out and race over to Fred's house.

"Okay, Sweetie-pie! But don't ruin your new suit!" yells Mom as I run off. "I love that suit and can't wait to take photos of you in it! It looks so good on you, my little yum-yum!"

Yikes!

I'm outside in this ridiculous suit again!

"Fred! Why are you dancing in your front yard?" I shout as I run up to him.

"It happened! The… wait… what are you wearing? It looks awful," Fred remarks. "You have bad taste in clothes, but this is a new low, even for you."

"It's not what you wear but how you wear it."

"Nobody could make that suit look good. Even LeBron James wouldn't look cool in those clothes. Even Will Smith would look terrible in that. Even Albert Einstein would look bad in that suit! Even-"

"Alright, alright. Never mind my clothes. What are you so happy about?" I change the subject quickly.

"There is a large comet coming directly to Earth! Well, I'm not sure that it is a comet. It could be a comet, or a meteor, or space junk, or a UFO! Maybe a flying saucer," Fred replies. "But whatever it is, it is coming directly this way. It is on target to hit somewhere close to our city. If I have calculated it correctly, it looks like it is coming straight to my house! I think it might be something that has responded to my message to outer space!"

"Whoa. That's totally cool."

"From my estimates, I think it is a comet that is being steered by an external force. Maybe an alien is driving the comet?"

"Wow. That is so crazy."

"Quickly, come inside and I'll show you. This might be it! This might be the moment that goes down in history!"

Full of excitement, we race upstairs to his room.

He shows me the view through his telescope. "Look!"

Wow!

He is right!

I see it!

There is a blurry flaming object approaching us!

It is getting bigger - fast!

Like, really fast.

"Wow! Fred, you discovered a comet! That is so cool! Because you discovered it, they are going to name it after you – 'Dumbo's comet'!" I laugh.

"No way. This will be my first discovery of many, so they'll call it 'Fred's Comet 1'. And the next one, they will call 'Fred's Comet 2!' And after that 'Fred's Comet 4'!"

"What about 'Fred's Comet 3?'"

"Hmm… no, 'Fred's Comet 3' is a silly name. Why would you even suggest that?" Fred says.

"Never mind," I shake my head.

"Remember this moment, Blake. This is a significant moment in time! This moment will go down in the history books. It will be remembered forever! Now, get out of my way, I want to look at my comet," Fred says as he pushes in on the telescope and refocuses.

"Uh-oh," Fred whispers as he stares at his discovery.

"What's wrong?"

"Uh, I have changed my mind. I don't want this named after me. Maybe they can name it after you," Fred says as he moves away from the telescope. "I don't want anything to do with that comet, Blake. It's nothing to do with me."

"Why? This is a great moment. You should be excited."

"This isn't a great moment, Blake. This is bad," Fred continues. "Really bad."

"What? Why? This is what you have hoped for all your life," I say. "You said that there could be alien life on that comet! This is what you wanted. You'll go down in history as the man who discovered life-forms from space! That's awesome! This is a time to be excited!"

Turning to the window, I watch as the comet steers through the sky and then crashes into the lake behind Fred's house!

It is so close to us!

Almost like it is coming directly to us.

This is so cool.

But Fred has gone pale white.

He should be happy, not scared.

"The comet…" Fred says slowly. "It wasn't a comet. It was a massive alien coming straight for us."

Oh no…

Chapter 5

I have a bad feeling about this…

Usually, I would be quite excited about a comet falling into the lake near Fred's house. That should be as exciting as ice-cream for breakfast.

But not this time.

This time, I am worried because the comet isn't a comet at all.

"Do you think it's friendly?" I say to Fred as we stare out of his window at the lake.

"I don't think so," Fred shakes his head. "It was massive, and it came straight here. It was clearly coming straight for our signal from the Intergalactic Communicator. That can't be good."

Fred scrambles over his machine and then pulls the plug out of the wall. After the machine has been turned off, he hides under his bed.

"What are you doing?"

"That alien has traced our signal. Now that the machine has been turned off, it won't be able to find us anymore."

"I thought this would be exciting for you? An alien has crashed into the lake, Fred. Like you said, this is a moment in history. We have to go down there and find out more."

"If we go down there, we will be history. A flaming alien, the size of a comet, has crashed into the lake behind my house," Fred says, still hiding under the bed. "That doesn't sound friendly. A friendly alien would have sent a message back saying, '*Hi. My name is Alan the Alien, and I liked your message. Thanks for being so friendly. Let's have a chat over a nice cup of alien tea. I have an alien brand of tea called 'Gravi-tea'.*' That would have been a friendly response. This wasn't friendly. This was trouble."

Just in case it is trouble, I take my official Ninja Spy uniform out of my backpack and slip it on.

"What are you doing?" Fred asks.

"We should go down there, Fred. We have to find out what has crashed into the lake. We can't bring something like that to Earth and then let it wander around unchecked. The lives of everyone in our city could be at stake now. We have to be prepared for the worst. This could be very dangerous."

"That's the reason we shouldn't go down there! Can't we just call the police?"

Shaking my head, I walk out of Fred's house wearing the Ninja Spy uniform, heading towards the lake. I am halfway to the lake when Fred catches up to me.

"I thought this was too dangerous for you?" I ask.

"It is," Fred is nervous. "But there is no way that I am letting you discover alien life before me. I mean, what would they call the alien if you found it? A 'Blakeatron'? I don't think so. 'Fredatron' sounds so much better."

"Shhh…"

Quietly, we walk to the lake where the comet crashed…

The lake looks calm.

There is no sign of life.

"Well, looks like nothing happened here. Time to go home," Fred states.

"Wait, Fred. Whatever fell into the lake must have sunk to the bottom."

"Oh well, there is no chance that we can find it now. It's at the bottom of the lake and will stay there forever. Forever. At least we tried," Fred states and turns around, clearly scared.

"Wait," I grab his arm. "We can't just walk away from this. We have to go in and look for it."

"Uh-uh. No way. Nope. Not a chance. I am not doing that. You are the one that is dressed as a Ninja Spy, so you can go into the water to find it. But they are still naming that alien after me."

"I'll go into the water and swim around. I'll search for any signs of life down there, but I need you to stay on the edge here and keep an eye out. If anything goes wrong, I want you to go to the Ninja Spy Agency and get Tekato. He is my trainer. He will know what to do."

Fred nods, "Ok Blake."

Just as I step my toe into the water, the lake starts to rumble…

Fred jumps behind me. "Oh no."

Slowly, something starts to rise to the surface of the water… and it is huge!

Now I see the eyes that Fred spoke of earlier! And then, there are some arms!

Lots of arms!

And a set of wings!

"It's a giant alien," Fred shouts. "A real alien!
Blake, an alien has crashed into Earth!"

Fred isn't scared anymore; he is excited!

But the giant alien looks annoyed.

He is staring at us like he wants to eat us alive.

"Careful, Fred. We don't know if he is
friendly-"

"Hello!" yells Fred. "I am Fred! I am a human from the planet Earth. I come in peace. I am so excited to meet you! You must have received the message that I sent into outer space. Is that why you are here?"

"Hello Fred," replies the giant alien in a deep, powerful voice. "I did intercept your message. Thank you for being so nice. We should have a cup of alien tea one day and discuss the big issues of the universe. However, that is not why I am here. I am here because I also intercepted another message sent from this location."

Oh man!

I hope it is not my message!

"I am looking for the greatest Ninja Spy of all time!" he yells.

Argh!

That is my message!

The alien looks straight at me wearing my Ninja Spy uniform.

"Are you Blake, the undefeated Ninja Spy?"

"Ah, yep," I mumble, looking up.

"My name is Moon Razor, and I am the greatest ninja in the universe," the alien states proudly. "I have battled hundreds of life-forms over thousands of years, and I am undefeated. I am unbeatable. Until yesterday, there was no doubt that I, Moon Razor, am the greatest ninja in the universe. All life-forms across the galaxies know that I am the ultimate ninja. I am the greatest!"

"Um… sure," I shrug.

"Then I received your message saying that you are the greatest. This cannot be."

"Um… like… so… we should just call it a draw and let there be two undefeated ninjas in the universe? Yep, that's what we should do."

"No! There cannot be two undefeated ninjas in the universe. I have made it my mission to come here and defeat you. We shall battle to decide who is truly the greatest ninja of all time."

Oh man, a ninja alien.

I thought a ninja ghost was bad, but this dude is a whole lot worse.

"Blake, what have you done?" Fred says to me, still staring at the alien.

"I have discovered aliens. I'll go down in history for this," I whisper.

"You will be history if you can't sort this out!"

Fred is right.

If Moon Razor is the greatest ninja alien in the universe, then I don't stand a chance against him. Time to use my massive intellect to sort this out.

"Mr. Moon Razor, sir, we shouldn't fight. We should be using our powers for good and not for fighting each other. It would be a waste of our ninja talents to combat each other," I say, scrambling for an idea to get out of this dilemma. "Ninja powers are very special, and we should be friends. We can even be best friends, if you would like."

"No. We cannot be friends. We must fight, Blake. I have made a bet with my friends that I will crush you. If I lose, I will be cleaning their stinky bathrooms for years! We must fight!" Moon Razor replies as he ties on a headband.

I couldn't imagine what an alien bathroom is like, but I do know that I wouldn't want to be cleaning it!

"Look, Mr. Razor, sir, I don't want to hurt you. I am super-tough and super-strong, and I don't want to damage your beautiful face," I lie, trying to get him to calm down.

"We fight now!" he yells.

Well, that didn't work.

"Why the rush? Can't we talk first?" I plea.

"No! We fight now! I must get back home before dinner. We are having intergalactic pizza."

Uh-oh.

How am I going to beat a ninja alien who is 50 stories tall?

Moon Razor could easily defeat me!

I need help from my friends at the Ninja Spy Agency, but I have to get past this guy first!

"Time to fight!" Moon Razor yells as he leaps from the lake and lands in front of me with a perfect crocodile stance.

Whoa, he's big.

Now that we are toe to toe on land, I realize what my next move must be…

Run!

I need to get out of here.

Just as I am about to turn around, Moon Razor sweeps one of his arms down in front of me - causing me to fly into the air!

Dodging his fist, I leap to the side of the lake.

But then he slams down another fist!

And another!

It must be easy to fight when you've got four arms. And probably easier to carry the shopping, but man, I'd have to buy more gloves.

"Hey Moon Face, you might have four arms, but I have forearms!" I yell.

"Do your forearms do anything?" Moon Razor looks at me confused.

Looking down at my forearms, I realize that they don't actually do much. "Um… no. Come to think of it, they don't do anything."

"And I have four forearms!" he yells and strikes another fist down.

Again, I dodge it.

As he pulls one of his fists out of the ground, I grab hold of his collar and pull myself up so that we are face to face.

"Hey Toon Razor, can you smell that? I ask.

"No?"

I fart in his face.

This is not a move I learned from the Ninja Spy Agency.

But they also didn't teach me what I should do when I encounter a giant ninja alien!

"Awk! You are disgusting! What have you been eating!?" Moon Razor yells.

As Moon Razor is cringing in disgust, I slap him in the face.

At least I can say I got one punch in before he flattens me.

"Fred! Run home!" I say as I use my chance to run away too. "Look at the trouble your experiment has caused!"

"What?! Do you think this is my fault!? This is your fault, Blake! You and your stupid boasting message to the galaxy! You've done this!"

"I haven't got time to argue the details, Fred! Hide in your house. I'll be at the Ninja Spy base!" I yell back.

Moon Razor loses sight of me while he is coughing and I charge towards Ninja Spy headquarters.

I need help defeating Moon Razor, otherwise I am toast!

Chapter 6

In a panic, I bust into Ninja Spy headquarters…

But there is nobody around.

Not a soul.

Where are they all?

This place is usually full of people buzzing around being ninjas. There are usually people hiding in the shadows, doing push-ups, studying and playing badminton. Ninjas love badminton.

Looking for anybody, I look into the training room – nobody.

The computer center – empty.

The tanning salon – not a soul.

Then I walk into the lunch room…

And find all the Ninja Spies eating fried chicken!

There is no panic at all!

"Everybody listen!" I holler. "There is a giant ninja alien here to fight me! He is going to destroy me! I need everybody to help me defeat this guy! All the ninjas with knowledge about how to defeat a giant ninja alien, please step forward!"

But everyone ignores me and continues eating.

"What is going on?" I ask Agent Lightning, one of my Ninja Spy training partners.

"It's Tekato's birthday, and we are having a party for him. Tekato's birthday is very important."

Tekato is my Ninja Spy trainer, and he has taught me some really awesome moves, like the eye-stare-knock-down. It is a move that takes a lot of work to master, but I can now knock someone over by staring at them continually for four hours straight.

"Did you hear what I said, Agent Lightning?" I ask.

"I heard what you said, Blake," Lightning sighs. "Here have some cake. That should cheer you up."

"That's not cake," I explain as Agent Lightning hands me a piece of fried chicken with a candle in it.

"It is a Kentucky Fried Cake. It's delicious. Tekato loves fried chicken."

"Have you heard what I said about the giant alien?" I ask again.

"Yeah, we all did."

"Well? Why is nobody coming to help me?" I ask.

"Blake," sighs Agent Lightning. "We are all a little tired of you telling everybody how you are undefeated and the greatest Ninja Spy of all time. It seems like you don't need our help. You have told us that you're so awesome that we think you could probably handle an alien ninja by yourself."

Well, this isn't fair.

More importantly, why was I not invited to Tekato's birthday party?

I need to find Tekato.

Looking in the gadget room, I find Tekato with a party hat on and enjoying his Kentucky Fried Cake.

The cake is huge!

"Tekato! Why didn't you invite me to your party?" I say as I approach him.

"Urrrr, I thought you were... washing your eyeballs with soap," Tekato gives me a poor excuse.

Maybe he is upset with my show-boating too. And why is everyone washing their eyeballs with soap?

"Whatever. I need your help! There is a giant ninja alien at the lake who wants to fight me! I accidently sent a message into outer space saying that I am the greatest ninja of all time and Moon Razor, the alien, intercepted the message. He thinks he is the greatest ninja of all time, and now he wants to prove it. What am I going to do?"

"Have some Kentucky Fried Cake?"

"This is no time for cake."

"Yes, yes. You are right. I have heard of those ninja aliens. I have read about them in the scrolls of our ancient ninja ancestors."

"And?"

"And they are the most dangerous ninjas in the universe. They have been known to battle hundreds of aliens at one time, while eating lunch! They are super talented ninjas," says Tekato. "If they want to fight you, you are doomed. They won't stop until you are completely destroyed."

"Argh! What do I do?" I ask.

"Hmmm…" Tekato puts his finger on his chin and thinks hard.

He thinks…

And he thinks…

And he thinks.

After about five minutes, I ask, "What are you thinking about?"

"I am considering how long it will take me to eat the rest of this Kentucky Fried Cake."

"No!" I exclaim. "You need to be thinking about how I can defeat the alien!"

"Oh yes. Of course. Well, to have any chance of defeating a ninja that size, you will need to be the same size," Tekato explains.

He points to the table in front of me.

That's it!

I'll eat all of his enormous Kentucky Fried Cake until I am the same size as the giant alien. What a great idea!

I race across to the table and start chomping down.

Within a few seconds of Ninja Spy power-eating, I have consumed pounds of Kentucky Fried Cake – and my Ninja Spy trousers rip open from my large butt!

"Blake! Stop! What are you doing?!" Tekato yells.

"I'm getting massive like you said," I answer with a mouth full of chicken.

"I pointed to the Magnify Machine behind the cake! I didn't point to the cake! Eating chicken won't make you grow taller! You need to use that machine to become the same size as the ninja alien."

That makes more sense.

"Find some trousers before you enlarge yourself too. You cannot go out fighting with your fat butt hanging out of your split ninja pants."

Oh no.

The only spare trousers I have are the ugly suit trousers my Mom bought for me.

But I have no choice! I put on the bad suit pants, shuffle over to the Magnify Machine, and turn it on.

Zap!

Within seconds, I am a giant!

I am 50 stories tall, the same size as the ninja alien!

"Blake!" Tekato yells. "Look what you have done!"

My body has grown through the roof of the Ninja Spy headquarters.

"You do not use the Magnify Machine inside! That is common sense!" screams Tekato. "You need to use it outside the building! It even says it on the instructions!"

"There were instructions?"

"Blake!"

I probably should have done this outside.

And boy, Tekato is mad.

"Hehe. It's a new skylight for the building. I always thought that there wasn't enough natural light coming into the place. Happy birthday?"

"You need to clean this up!" he yells.

"I haven't got time to help clean up. I have a ninja alien to fight," I answer. "I'll meet you on the corner of Walk and Don't Walk Street after I fight with the alien. Bring the Magnify Machine to shrink me back to normal size."

"Blake, those aren't the names of the streets! They are the pedestrian crossing lights on the traffic stops."

"What do you mean?"

"*Sigh*, never mind," Tekato shakes his head.

Chapter 7

Supersized, I race across the city to the lake outside Fred's house.

Wow. I can run so much quicker now that my legs are the size of a tall building. Maybe I should do this before the next school athletic carnival?

When I arrive at the lake, all I can hear is Fred's laughter.

I look down at him.

"Ha ha ha! Nice outfit, elite Ninja Spy," Fred is laughing as he points at my trousers. "You know, for a Ninja Spy, you are not very discreet. Shouldn't you be hiding in shadows and stuff?"

"Fred, I had no choice but to wear these trousers," I explain. "I ripped my tactical ninja trousers. But it's ok; no one will notice me. It is the way of the Ninja Spy not to be seen."

"At least now your head matches the size of your ego," Fred bellows.

Suddenly I hear a rupture of laughter.

Looking down, I see everyone in town laughing at the way I'm dressed.

I guess being a giant ninja is not a good way to go unnoticed.

As I look at the crowd, I see Amy laughing so much that she is crying!

Luckily, she does not know who I am in my awesome disguise.

"Ah, welcome to the battle of your life, Ninja Spy," the deep voice comes from behind me. "Now it is time to find out who is the greatest ninja in the universe. And I'll give you a clue: it's me."

It is Moon Razor; he has found me.

But I guess I wasn't hard to find at this size.

"That's not a clue," I respond. "That's an answer."

"Well… nice trousers," Moon Razor laughs.

"Yeah. I hold them up with my belt… my **asteroid belt!**" I joke.

"I don't get it," Moon Razor looks confused.

"It's… oh, don't worry," I shrug.

"We must fight now, ninja human. I must defeat you in a battle to the end. Once I have defeated you, I will remain the greatest ninja in the entire universe. Only one of us is going home undefeated, and that is me!" Moon Razor looks furious.

"You have dared to challenge me, and now you are going to feel the full force of my powers!"

"Not today, Moon Blade. You are not going to beat me. You are going home to your planet. And I am going to be the one that sends you there!"

"My name is Moon Razor!"

Moon Razor picks up a car and flings it at me!

Yikes!

I duck under it and grab a truck. I check no one is in it, then hurl it at my opponent.

But he whacks it away with a bus!

This dude is totally tough. Maybe he really is the greatest ninja in the universe?

Moon Razor runs towards me with four arms opened wide!

I duck one of his punches but then he pushes me with another one of his arms!

Falling backwards, I land on a block of buildings!

Ouch!

That hurts!

Slowly, I get back on my feet and see what I fell on - a new building that hasn't been completed yet, an old building that was due to be knocked down tomorrow and…

Argh! I crushed my favorite comic book store too!

Moon Razor charges towards me with a second phase attack.

He unleashes a barrage of punches, but I am able to block them.

One of his punches misses me and smashes the top of the town clock tower!

We start to fight across town, destroying a lot of homes and buildings along the way. We scuffle across the landscape, exchanging elite ninja moves.

"Get out of the way!" I shout to all the little people beneath my feet.

I make extra sure not to crush anyone while defending myself against Moon Razor.

But then…

Whack!

Chapter 8

Moon Razor slams me with a triple fisted punch attack and I go flying over the buildings, landing in the forest.

Ouch.

These trees hurt when you land on them!

Oh no.

Here comes Moon Razor again...

Doesn't this guy ever give up?

"Look, Mr. Moon Shaver, let's just say that I am the greatest Ninja in the universe and be done with all this fighting. We can discuss the matter further over a glass of orange juice. We can discuss other matters as well, like the use of hair. Clearly, you don't have any hair, so I will explain the use of hair to you. It's great for fashion-"

"No! And my name is Moon Razor, not Moon Shaver!"

Whoops.

He looks extra angry now.

I jump back up on my feet and defend myself against his attacks.

He swings another punch.

I defend it.

Another punch.

And I block it.

He keeps punching, and I keep defending...

And defending...

And defending!

This guy is so fast that I can't do anything but defend against his punches!

Finally, he takes a breath.

I take the chance to run away. I have to think of a new plan!

Nothing I am doing is working. There has to be some sort of way to beat this guy!

Moon Razor chases me, and we are covering miles in just seconds because of our size.

Unfortunately, I run straight back into somebody's house…

Whoops.

Luckily, there was nobody inside.

"Now, it is time to be defeated!" announces Moon Razor.

"No way, Moon Face!" I yell back.

"Moon Razor!" he shouts.

"Ok, Mr. Moon Blazer!"

"Moon Razor!"

"It's time to finish this, Moon Laser!"

"You're right, Ninja Spy! It is time for me to finish this! You will not be able to defend yourself against the might of the alien ninja star!"

That's where he is wrong.

I have been practicing my ninja star catches all week!

Admittedly, I haven't caught one yet, but I am confident that I can catch this one!

He throws the ninja star…

Yes!

I grab it!

I flick the ninja star behind me and plan my next attack.

Hearing a plane fly over my head, I jump high into the clouds…

Yes! I grab the wings, taking a ride on the jet.

"Turn around!" I shout to the pilot.

He does. I guess most people will do what you ask when you are 50 stories tall. Maybe I should ask for school to be canceled once this is all over?

Hanging onto the plane, I travel through the thick, gray clouds.

Moon Razor doesn't know where I am.

I see a chance, and let go of the plane, gliding through the air towards Moon Razor!

As I emerge from the cloud, I am able to complete a secret ninja move that is centuries old - a hammer-time kick!

Slam!

Moon Razor goes flying through the air and is defeated!

It's my ultimate finishing move.

Nobody has ever been able to withstand the power of my hammer-time kick.

Nobody.

But as I approach the fallen alien, he starts to get back to his feet!

What?!

He was able to withstand my ultimate attack!

Oh no!

I don't have any other ninja moves that can defeat him!

"Is that the best you've got?" he says as he walks back towards me.

"Um... yep," I shrug. "Yep. That is the best I've got."

"Ha ha!" he laughs. "Your best is not good enough to defeat me. I am the greatest ninja in the universe. I am undefeated!"

"Ok," I say.

"No, I… wait, what?"

"Sure. You're the greatest ninja in the universe. Congratulations. Well done. Hooray. Now get out of here," I say, hoping that he will leave.

"Great! Now, I own your planet. This is my planet now. I am now the master of planet Earth! I will use it for gardening and growing giant cabbages."

"What?" I question. "What are you talking about? You didn't say that when we started fighting!"

"Those are the rules which govern the universe. Everyone knows that. It is Universe Rule Number 14.6: *When an alien eats ice-cream standing upside down, the alien will remain upside down for a period of ten hours and...* no, wait. That's not the right rule," Moon Razor ponders his thoughts for a few moments. "It is Universe Rule Number 14.7: *When the planet's best ninja is defeated, the planet then belongs to the winning ninja!* And I am the winning ninja! This planet belongs to me! I own it!"

Oh man.

I can't let him win now.

"Well, this fight isn't over yet!" I yell.

"You just said it was."

"It was a ninja trick. I was only making you think that the fight is over so that I have enough time to plan my next move. This fight is still on Moon Foot, and I am still the greatest ninja in the universe," I say. "This planet does not belong to you!"

But how am I going to defeat him?

He is almost unstoppable!

What can I do to stop him?

And now he looks extra angry.

I'm doomed…

Then I remember what my Mom said!

"If you ever get into a fight with an alien, just remember that you can lasso them and then throw them into outer space."

I hate to admit it, but she might be right!

But what can I lasso him with?

We are giants, and there won't be any giant rope lying around…

Then I spot the power-lines that run through our town - they are perfect!

But if I touch the power-lines, I will be electrocuted!

Finally, I see some of the ninjas from the Ninja Spy Agency. They must have come to help!

"Quick, turn off the power-station!" I yell to my ninja friends. They move really, really slowly after I yell at them. It must have been all that Kentucky Fried Cake.

Moon Razor attacks me again, and I block punch after punch until I finally get the thumbs up from one of the other ninja spies. They have turned off the power.

Great!

Grabbing the power-lines below me, I swing them around my head.

"What are you doing? Cowboys use lassos, not ninjas. Are you a cowboy ninja now?" Moon Razor laughs. "A Cow-ja? Ha ha! Or maybe you will practice Kung Moo! Ha ha! Get it? *Kung* Fu and *Cow*-boy. Kung Moo! Ha ha ha!"

Yeesh. And I thought my jokes were bad. If the jokes are this bad, I am never going to an alien ninja comedy night.

While Moon Razor is laughing at his own jokes, I swing the lasso power-line in his direction.

It hits him!

"Yeeh-ha!" I yell.

"What?" Moon Razor looks surprised as he is wrapped up.

"It's time to go home, Moon Butt!"

I swing him around and around and around…And then I let go!

"Stay off my planet!" I yell as I throw Moon Razor back into space.

"You were lucky this time!" he screams as he disappears into the sky.

As soon as he is out of sight, I step across to Fred's home and lean into his bedroom window. I take his Intergalactic Communicator and point it at the sky.

"Moon Razor has been defeated! I'm still the greatest Ninja Spy in the cosmos!" I announce to the galaxy. "No one can beat me!"

"Blake! Have you learned nothing!?" lectures Fred from the window.

Chapter 9

Phew!

Giant alien ninja warrior – defeated!

"Blake, it's time to shrink back down to normal size," Tekato yells from the ground. "You can't stay giant forever. You have to come back to the Magnify Machine, and I will put it in reserve to shrink you back to normal size."

"Oh, ok," I reply. "But I just want to go for one last run as a giant."

"No, Blake-"

But I run off before Tekato has finished his sentence.

Quickly, I find the store where Mom buys all my hideous suits from - 'Ridiculous Men's Fashion'.

I crush it under my foot.

It was an accident, if anyone asks. I tripped, and accidently squashed it.

"Blake!" Tekato yells again. "Come back so we can use this machine! You cannot be a giant any longer!"

"Alright, alright. Here I come."

Tekato brings the machine out and presses all sorts of buttons.

Then…

Ping!

A laser hits me, and I shrink back to normal size.

"You are very lucky you survived this encounter, Blake," explains Tekato. "You have battled the greatest ninja in the universe, and you are still alive. Luck was on your side today. Let's hope that Moon Razor does not return for a rematch. You were brave and strong of heart, but you were not well behaved. You will be punished by doing one thousand push-ups every morning for the next year."

"Punished? But I just saved the world!" I complain.

"You broke almost every rule of the Ninja Spy," Tekato continues. "You exposed yourself as a Ninja Spy to the world. You fought another ninja simply for competition. You are not humble about your achievements. Plus, your rumble with the ninja alien has caused a lot of damage to the town, including our own headquarters."

"Aw man. One thousand push-ups every morning? Come on, can't I just eat worms for breakfast instead?"

"No Blake. Discipline is the trademark of a great ninja. You are very talented, but you still have a lot to learn in the way of the ninja. To become the best Ninja Spy you can be, you still have a lot of training to do."

"I'm sorry, Tekato, sir. I still have a lot to learn. I promise I'll try to follow the way of the Ninja Spy more closely," I say. "But I did get you a birthday present."

I hand Tekato the alien's large ninja star with a bow around it.

"Wow! This will be quite a collector's item!" smiles Tekato. "Thanks Blake."

Epilogue

The following day at school, I sit next to Amy in math class.

Amy is brilliant at math, and I usually talk to her about finding the right answers. But after she saw me in that horrible suit yesterday, I don't think she will ever talk to me again.

"Hi Blake," she smiles sweetly, as I sit down.

Well, this is a surprise!

Amy is talking to me, even after she saw me in that ugly suit.

"Um… err… ah…" I mumble.

"You can say hi," she giggles.

"That's it! That's what I want to say," I smile.

"Hi Amy."

"You're not wearing that silly suit today?"

"Um, no. My Mom made me wear that suit. She makes me do a calendar each year and she chooses the suits that I should wear for the photos. Every year, her fashion choices seem to get worse," I say, still embarrassed.

"Mine does the same," Amy says.

"Really?!"

"Shhh… don't tell anyone," she continues.

"But my Dad chooses my clothes for the calendar and last year he made me dress up as a giant broccoli. Can you believe that? Broccoli. I mean, what's he trying to say – 'Healthy but weird'? He made me dig a hole in the backyard and then sit in it for the photos. That was one of the worst experiences of my life."

I chuckle, "One year, my Mom made my Dad dress up like a spider. But my Mom is scared of spiders, so every time he came into the room, she would run away screaming!"

Amy laughs. I like her laugh.

"Did you see the giant ninja and alien fight yesterday?" she asks.

"Um, no," I reply. "Does anyone know who the brave ninja was?"

"I think the ninja had a very 'ridiculous' taste in clothes," Amy winks. "In fact, his trousers were **out of this world**…"

The End

12007982R00059